Merry Christmas, BIG HUNGRY BEAR!

by DON and AUDREY WOOD
illustrated by DON WOOD

SCHOLASTIC INC.
New York Toronto London Auckland Sydney
Mexico City New Delhi Hong Kong Buenos Aires

This book was originally published in hardcover by the Blue Sky Press in 2002.

ISBN 0-439-70820-6

12 11 10 9 8 7 6 5 4 3 2 1 4 5 6 7 8 9/0

Printed in the U.S.A. 40

First Scholastic paperback printing, September 2004

Dedicated to
Alejandra Demers

Hello, little Mouse.
I see you're ready
for Christmas.

My goodness!
What a lot of presents.
Are they all for you?

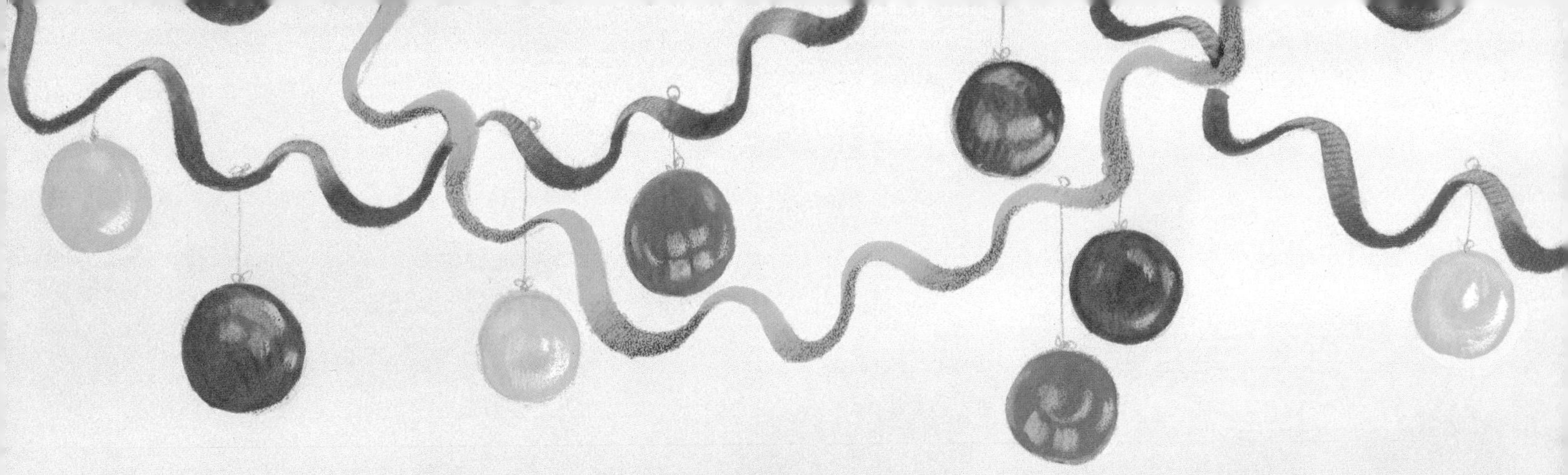

But, little Mouse,
what about the
big, hungry Bear
in the cold, dark
cave at the top
of the hill?

Ohhh, how
that Bear loves
Christmas presents!

Red ones, green ones,
little ones, big ones . . .

. . . that Bear would do ANYTHING
to get some presents.

But he never does.
Not even from Santa Claus.

BOO, HOO, HOO.
Every Christmas he sits alone
in his cold, dark cave, and
PLOP, PLOP, PLOP,
tears fall from his
big, hungry eyes.

Little Mouse,
what are you doing?

Oh, I see. What a brave
little Mouse you are.

No one else in the whole wide world
would go to the cold, dark cave
of the big, hungry Bear . . .

. . . especially on Christmas Eve.

Shhh, little Mouse.
Someone big is fast asleep. . . .

Quick,
little Mouse.
Someone big is
waking up. . . .

HIDE, LITTLE MOUSE!
SOMEONE BIG
IS PEEKING!

Come out, come out, little Mouse.
I see something big . . .

. . . for you!
MERRY CHRISTMAS . . .

. . . FROM THE BIG, HUNGRY BEAR!

The End